ROBOT RUNWAY®
FASHION COLORING BOOK

Illustrated by Justin J.Countee

Hi, I'm Captain Sheriff!!
This book belongs to:

Welcome to the exciting Robot Runway® universe!!

Immerse yourself in a world of robots and fashion with our captivating coloring book.

From sleek and futuristic bots to charming retro-inspired robots, this book contains over 50 unique illustrations to bring your creative visions to life. This coloring book for all ages is perfect for unleashing your artistic side in a fantastic robot-filled universe inspired by Science, Technology, Engineering, Art, and Math (STEAM).

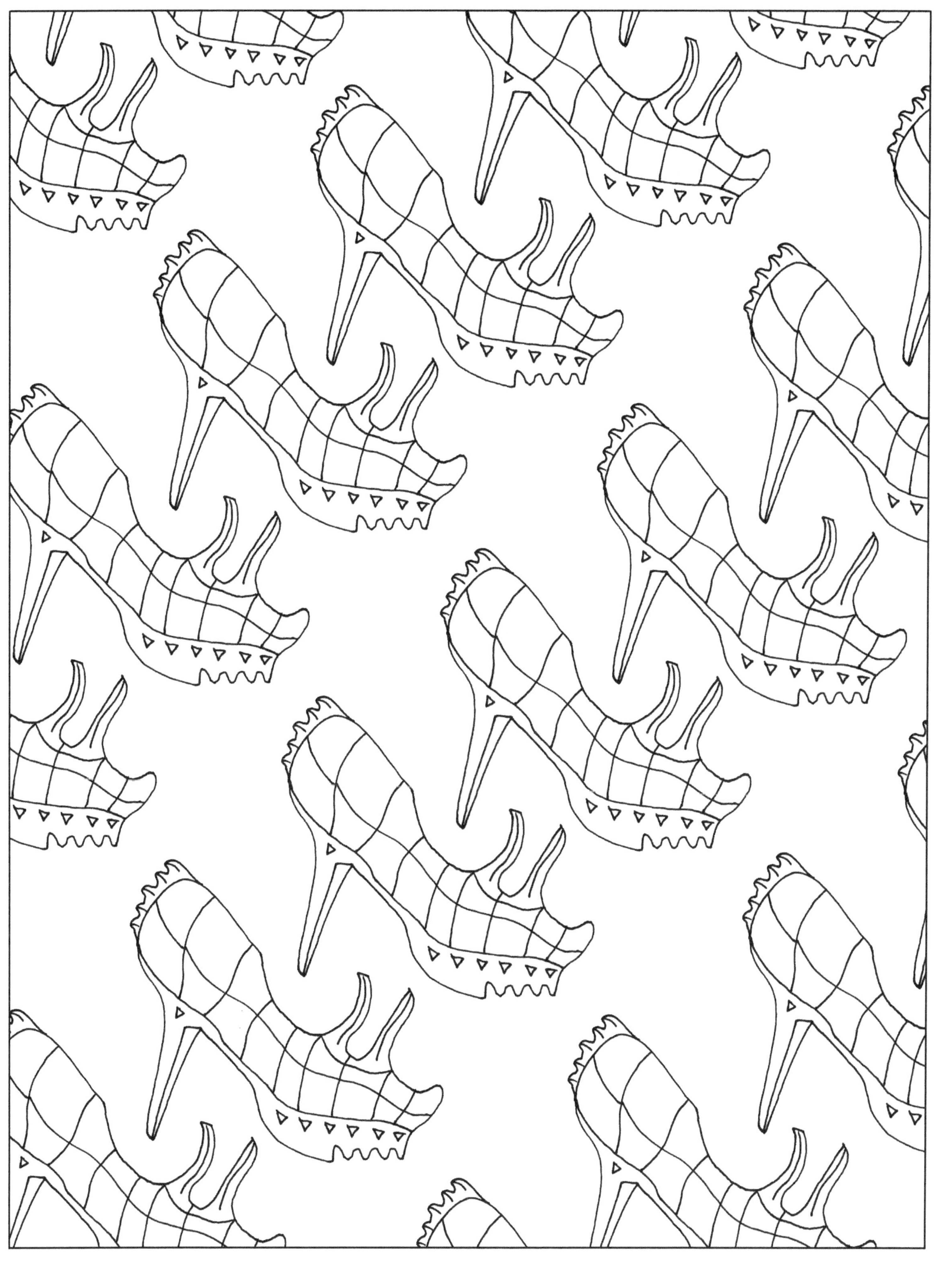

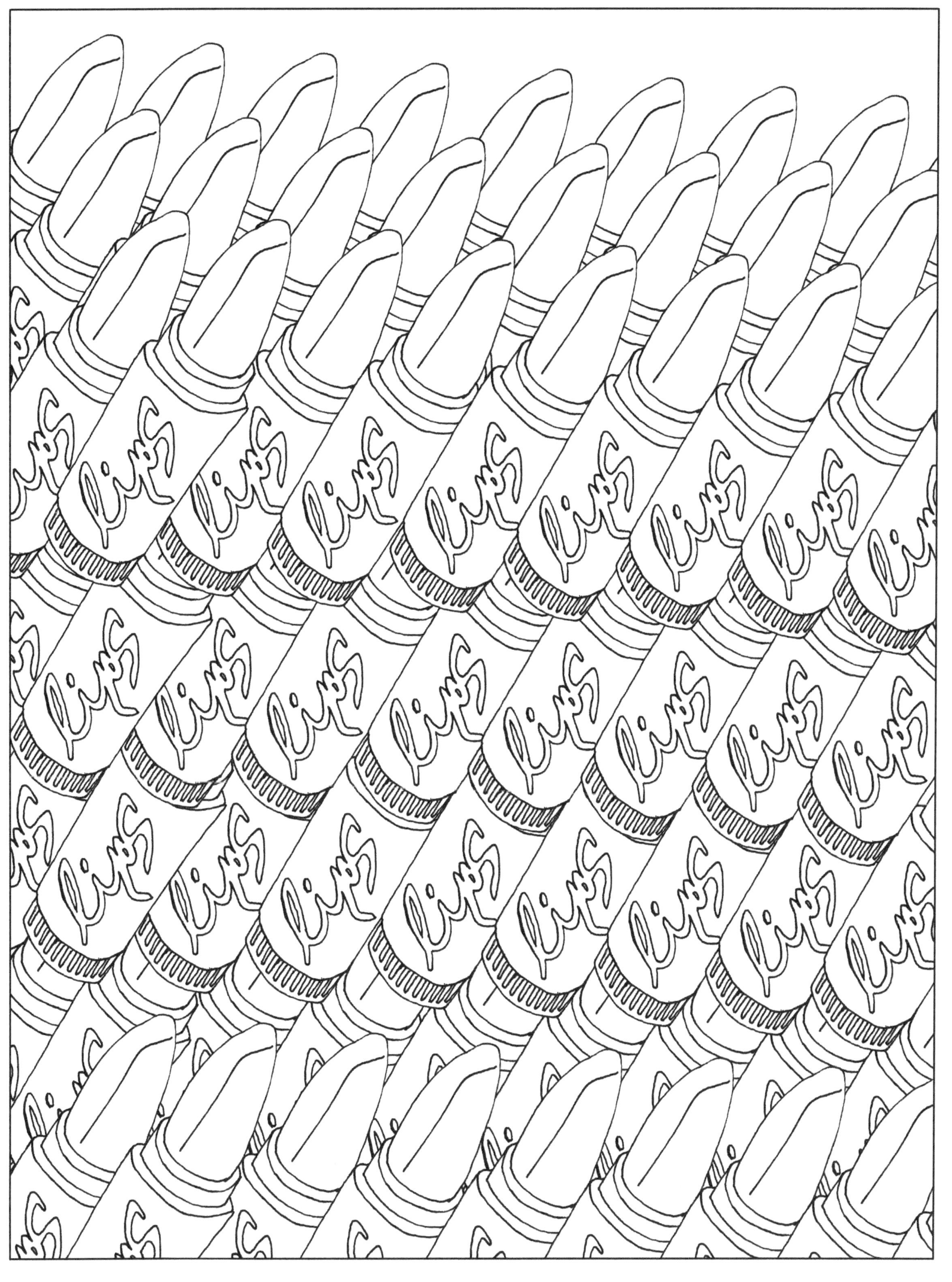

Me Me Me

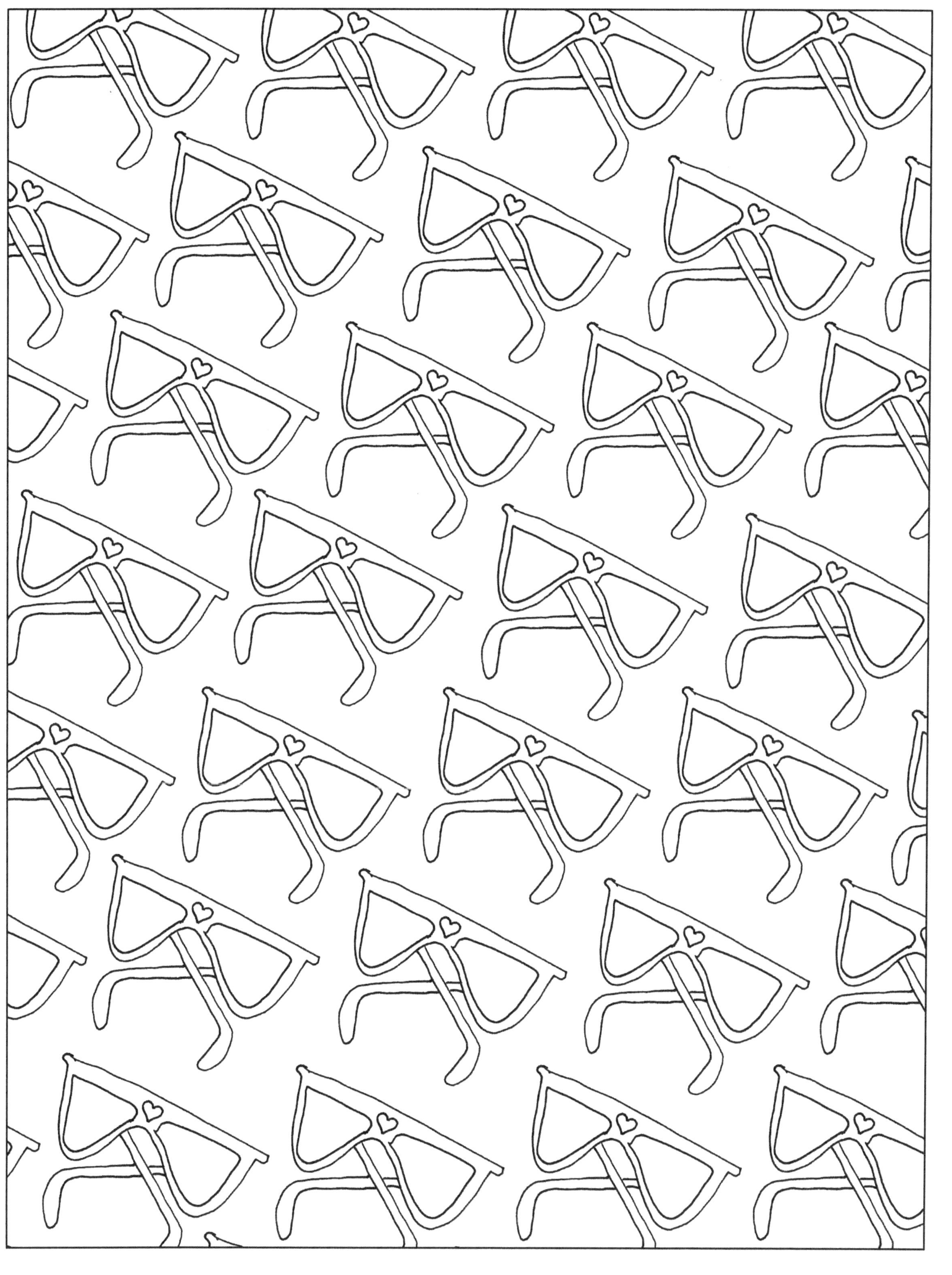

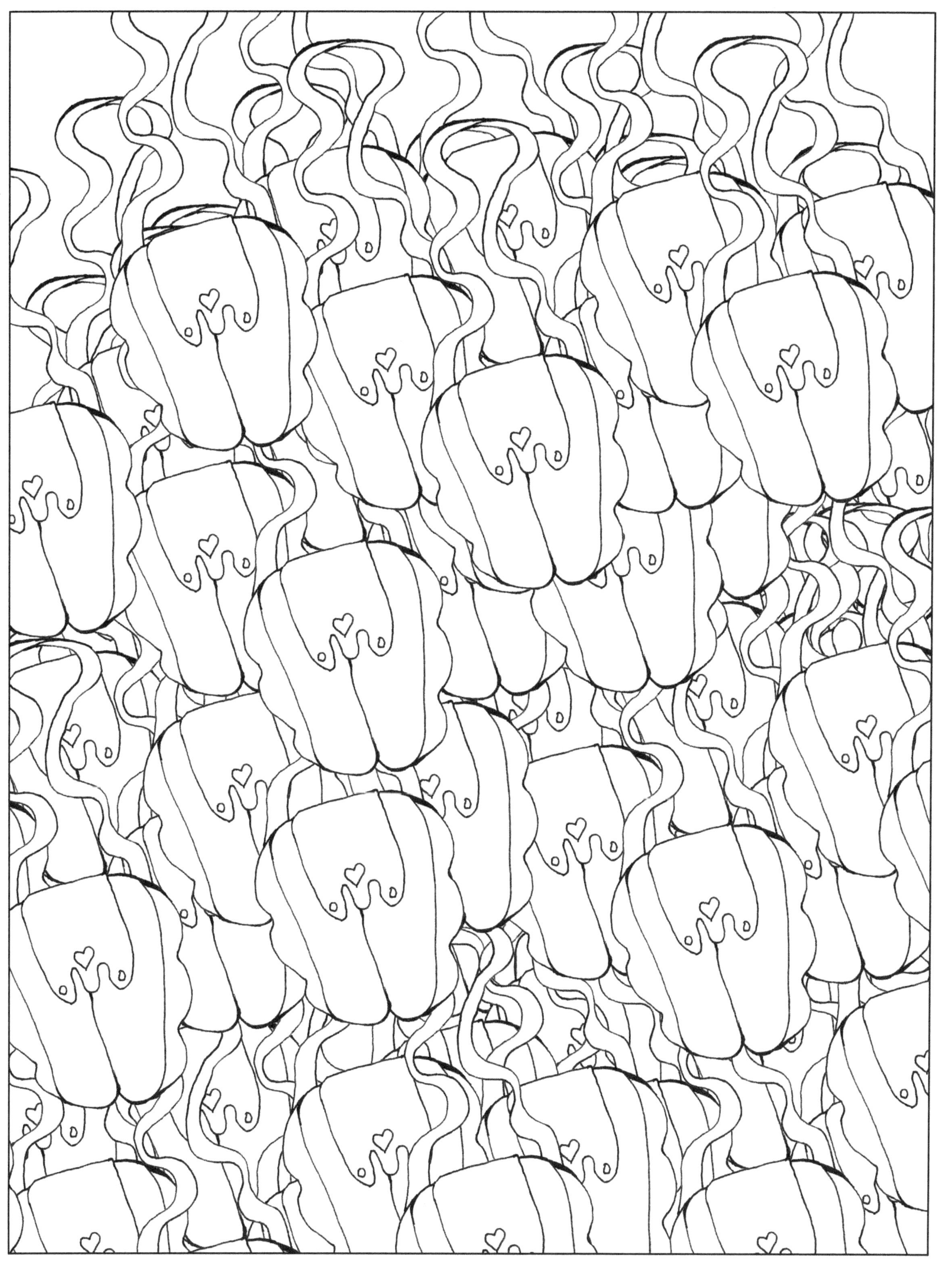

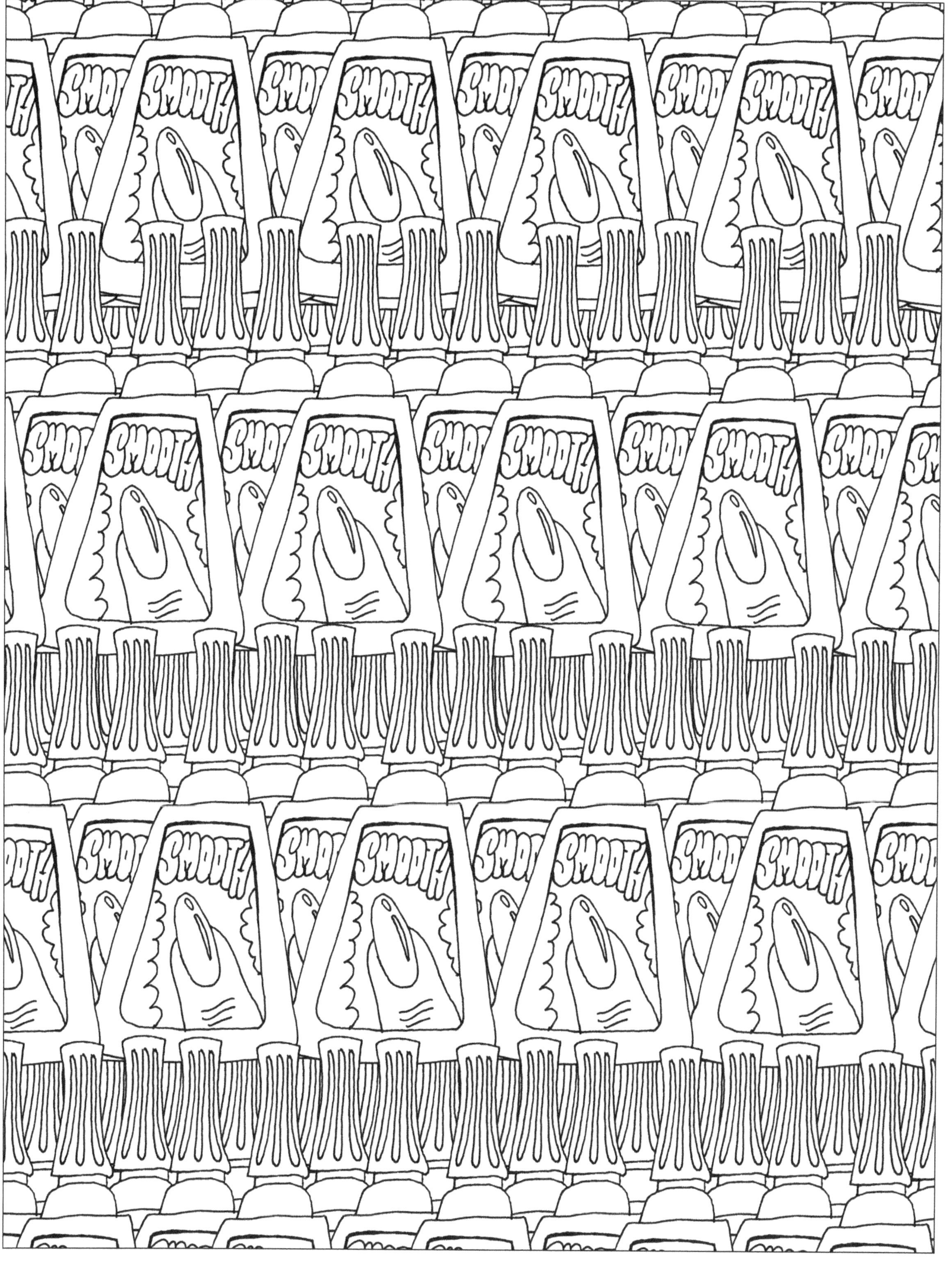
SMOOTH

Sassy
Classy

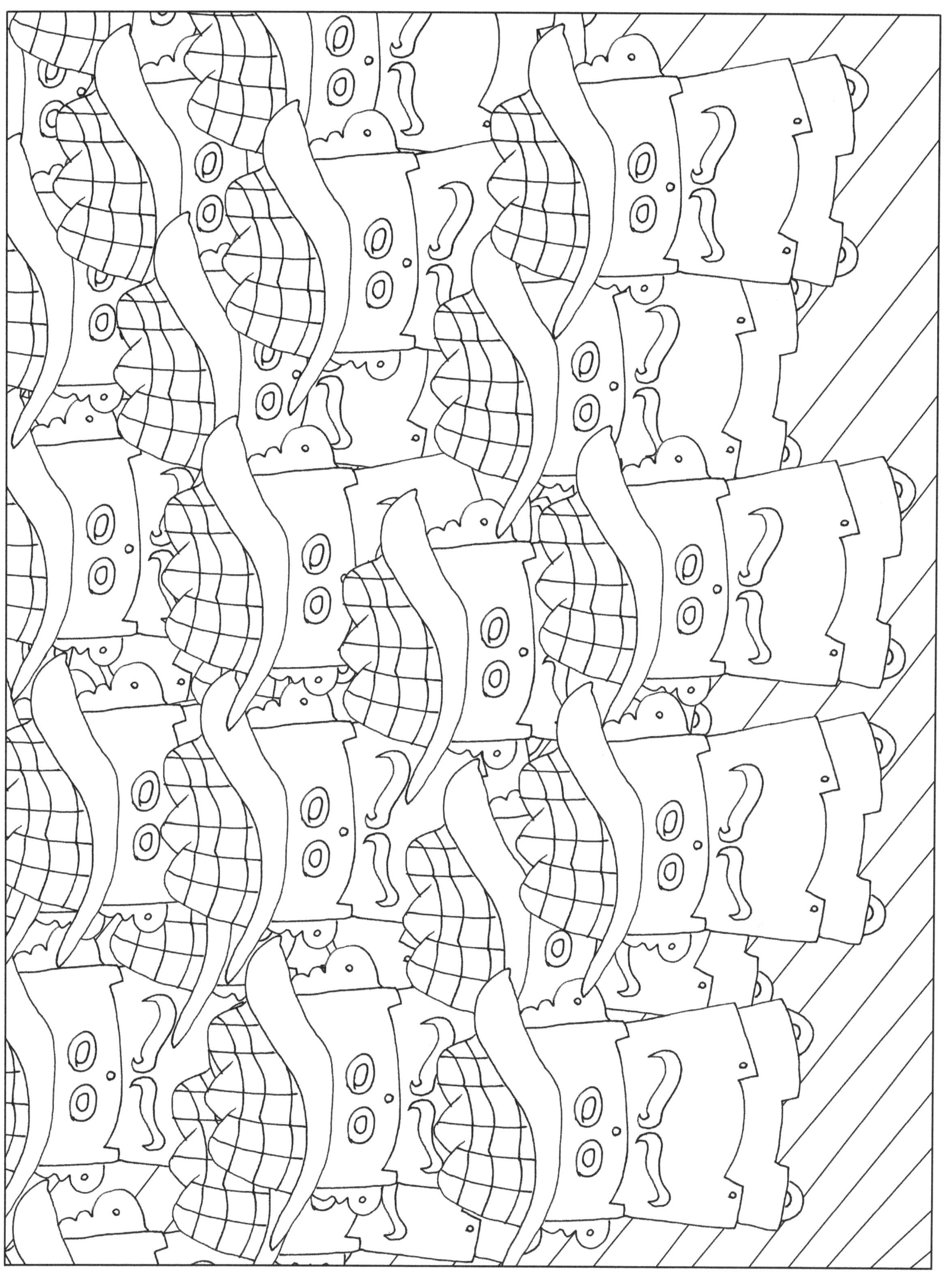

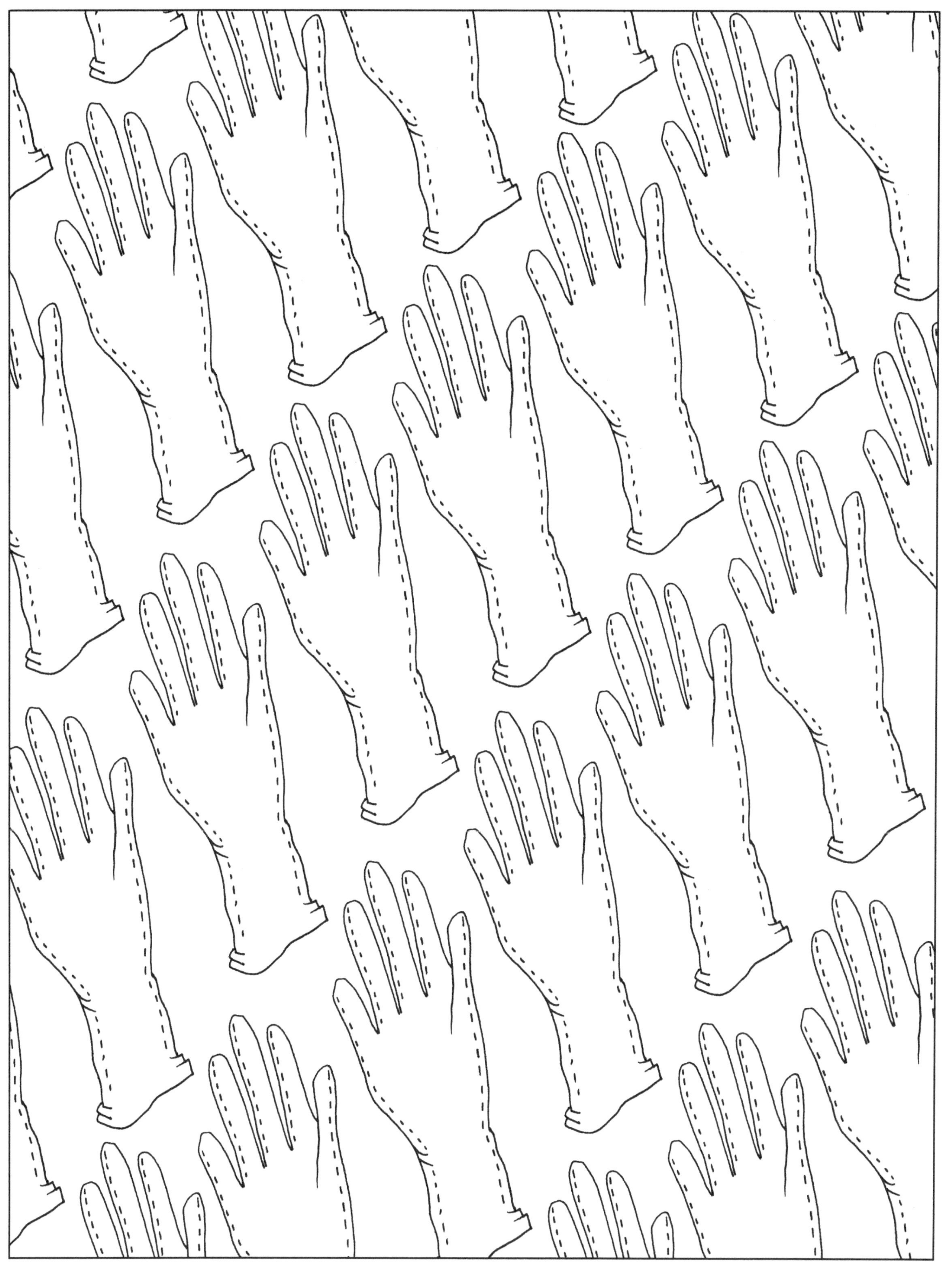

ROBOTS
★ARE★
S+T+E+A+M
Science
Technology Art
Engineering
Math

Plush

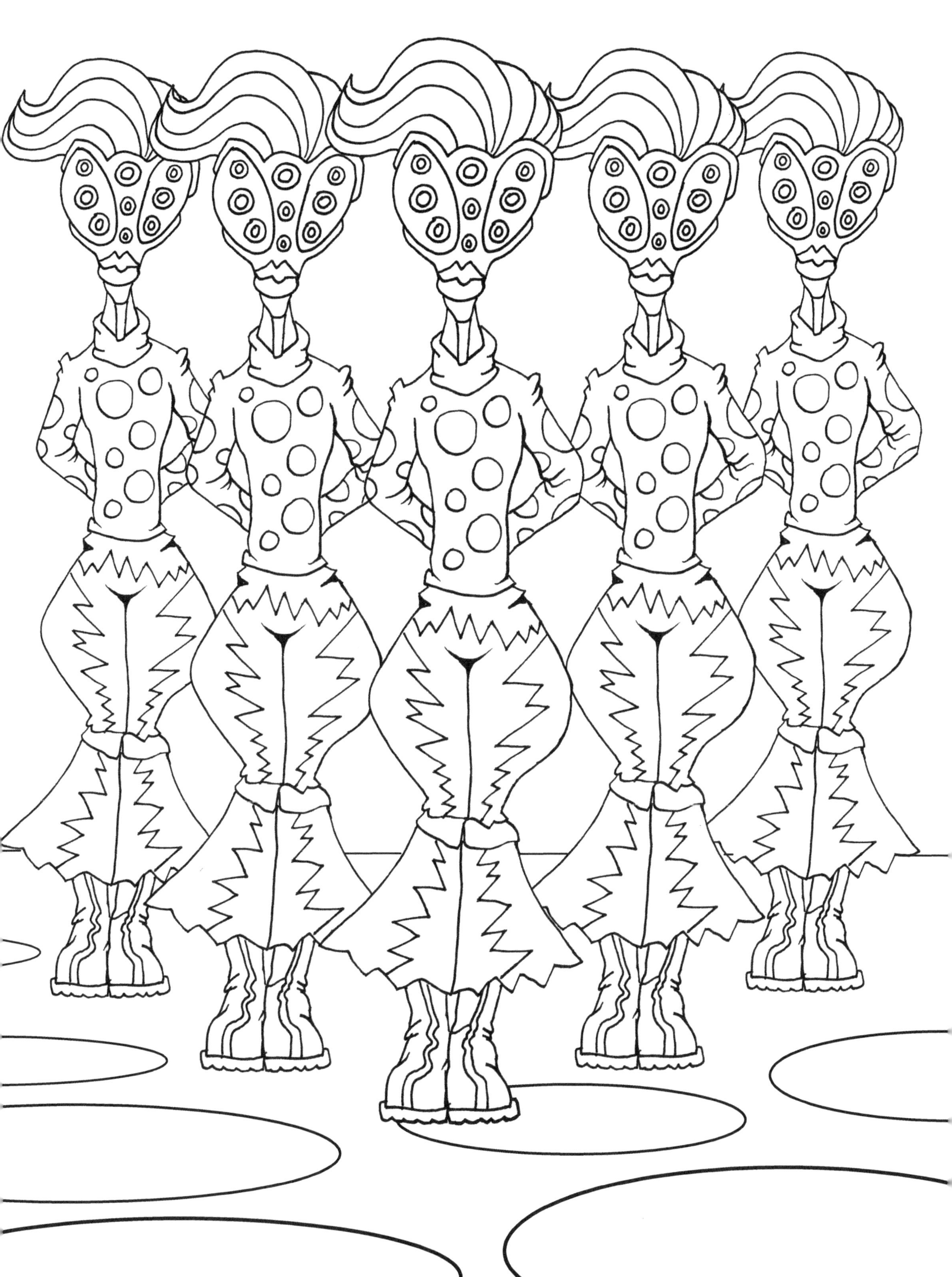

Hi, I'm Captain Sheriff! Be sure to post your finished art online!!
Just tag your art with #robotrunway on your favorite social media site!
Check out our cool Robot Runway® merch & entertainment at www.robotrunwayuniverse.com
Also check us out on:
YouTube
YouTube.com/@RobotRunway